LITTLE DERMOT AND THE THIRSTY STONES

told and illustrated by

RICHARD BENNETT

A collection of old tales retold must grow and ripen slowly to have lasting value and the ring of the true story-teller. Of how this collection of eight stories has been made, the author says:

"When I was a very small boy in Ireland, three-and-a-half-years old to be exact, I first heard the story of *Donaleen and Joanleen.* All I could remember about it was that someone was dragging a door along a rocky road and that my grandmother laughed very loudly while she told the tale.

"In 1926, on my first visit to the land of my birth, I heard the tale again, and since I have always been interested in folk art and folk ways I decided to make a collection of tales from the region of County Cork and County Kerry. On my many visits to Ireland between 1926 and 1949 I added to my collection. The task wasn't too difficult since there was a movement afoot in Ireland, sponsored by the government, to collect all the folk literature of the island. It was started in the public schools. Every child brought a story to class and used it as a composition subject. The best of these tales were sent to Dublin, where they again went through a process of careful selection and editing.

"This method at times had its amusing results. Since every child had to bring a story to school at least once a week and since there wasn't enough material to go around, a very resourceful character who lived in my village was called upon. He would make up a story on the spur of the moment. When it became known that I was also in search of such material, I often became the target of the resourceful story teller's art.

"In the early '40's I ran across two fascinating books in the New York Public Library: Keightley's *The Fairy Mythology* and Croker's *Fairy Legends and Traditions of the South of Ireland,* both first published early in the 19th century. In these I found many of the tales I had heard in Ireland in so many varied forms. With the help of these two scholarly volumes and my own research in Ireland, I have written in my own words the stories of this collection."

Mary Gould Davis, who read the stories in manuscript, reported: "With Mr. Bennett's drawings they should be very welcome in both public and school libraries and for home reading. The children will want to read them for themselves and they will have definite value to storytellers."

LITTLE DERMOT AND THE THIRSTY STONES

And Other Irish Folk Tales

Richard Bennett.

LITTLE DERMOT
and the Thirsty Stones

AND OTHER IRISH FOLK TALES

WRITTEN AND ILLUSTRATED BY

Richard Bennett

COWARD-McCANN, INC. NEW YORK

The author is grateful to the editors of *Story Parade* magazine for their permission to reprint four of the stories in this volume which first appeared in *Story Parade*.

Library of Congress Catalog Card No. 53-5228

PRINTED IN THE UNITED STATES OF AMERICA

BY THE MURRAY PRINTING CO., WAKEFIELD, MASSACHUSETTS

CONTENTS

LITTLE DERMOT
AND THE THIRSTY STONES

And Other Irish Folk Tales

DONALEEN AND JOANLEEN

ONCE UPON a time when pigs were swine and little birds built their nests in old men's beards, there lived in Ireland a little man and his wife and their names were Donaleen and Joanleen.

Their cabin stood at the foot of a high mountain and it was the cosiest cabin you could find in a long day's journey.

Every day Donaleen hitched his donkey to the cart and went off to his work—one day to the fields, another to the bog and, now and then, around the mountain to give a helping hand to a neighbor.

Joanleen spent the day minding the cabin and feeding her ducks and geese and planning little surprises to please her Donaleen. They had been married only a week and Joanleen was trying very hard to be a good little wife and make Donaleen the happiest of men. It was that fond of him she was. Yet I am sorry to say she didn't always use her head, as the old saying goes—but that is the gist of my story.

One bright summer day while Donaleen was hitching his donkey to the cart, he said to Joanleen, "Today is Friday and I would like a tasty bit of fish for my dinner."

"Very well," said Joanleen. "Fish it is." So Donaleen slapped the lines over the donkey's back and set off to the bog. He was no sooner out of sight than Joanleen filled her basket with duck eggs, wrapped her shawl about her head, and set off west the road. When she reached the village she sold her eggs in short order for a fair enough price and, with the money in her pocket, walked up to an old woman who kept a fish stall in one corner of the square.

"I want to buy some fish for my husband's dinner," said Joanleen. "Something nice and tasty."

"Tasty, is it?" said the old woman. "Well, now, these sprats are the very thing. A tastier fish never came out of the sea," and she pointed to a plate full of little fish in one corner of the stall.

"Very well," said Joanleen. "And how will I cook them?"

"Oh, they are such little fish," said the old woman. "They will scarcely need any cooking at all. Just show them to the fire."

So Joanleen paid for the fish, placed them in her basket, and set off east the road. When she reached her own door, she caught a glimpse of Donaleen coming around the mountain, so she quickly set the table and stirred up the fire. Remembering what the old fish woman had said, she carefully took each little fish out of the basket and held it steady for a moment before the blaze.

"Take a good look now," said Joanleen to each little fish. "Donaleen likes his fish nice and tasty."

When Donaleen sat down to his dinner of fish a few minutes later, I needn't tell you what happened. He had no sooner stuck his fork into the raw slippery fish when off onto the table they went and from there to the floor. The cat and dog made off with them in short order, I can tell you, and at that poor Joanleen threw her apron over her head and began to cry. Oh, there was great wailing, you may be sure, but as Donaleen was a kindly little man, he had Joanleen smiling again in no time at all.

"There, there," said he. "I haven't much liking for sprats

anyway. Now, tomorrow, you will cook me a nice dinner of ham and cabbage."

"Very well," said Joanleen, "ham and cabbage it is. And how will I cook it?" Oh, she was going to be very careful this time.

"No trouble at all," said Donaleen. "Just put the ham in with a head of cabbage."

That seemed easy enough, so that very evening Joanleen took the only ham in the house and went out into the garden. When she found a nice solid cabbage head, she cut a big hole in the very heart of it and placed the ham in the hole. That night, as luck would have it, a fox was prowling around that way and made off with the ham in short order. The next day when Donaleen came home for his dinner, he found Joanleen sitting on the hob with her apron over her head and crying for all she was worth.

Now Donaleen had spent the good part of the day working up a big appetite and when he found no sight of a dinner on the table, it didn't put him in the best of humor. After much coaxing, however, Joanleen told her story, but I am sorry to say Donaleen wasn't quite as soft-hearted this time and promptly lost his temper. Indeed, he took it so badly, he went off to work on Monday morning with a very sour expression on his face. Poor Joanleen was so upset. She

made up her mind, then and there, she would have such a pleasant surprise waiting for him that evening that he would be all smiles before the day was over.

Now, as luck would have it, a tinker came by that day with the finest array of pots and pans Joanleen had ever seen in her life. Indeed, she was fairly dazzled with the brightness of them.

"Any pots or pans today, ma'am?" said the old tinker, twisting them in his hand so that they twinkled brighter than ever in the sunlight.

"How much are they?" said Joanleen, blinking her eyes.

"And how much have you got?" said the old tinker.

"Wait now," said Joanleen, lifting a loose stone from the hearth where Donaleen kept his money. "Is this enough?" said she, holding up a little leather sack filled with gold and silver coins.

"Enough indeed, ma'am, enough indeed," said the old tinker, tossing the pots and pans on the table and making off west the road with the sack of Donaleen's money safe in his greatcoat pocket.

Joanleen had a grand time that day hanging the shiny pots and pans all over the dresser and singing to herself in high glee. She was that pleased. Indeed, she could hardly wait to see the expression Donaleen would have on his face when he saw the fine shiny array. There was no doubt about it. Joanleen was sure she had made a great bargain.

When it finally was time to prepare dinner, she made a good fire on the hearth and then went out to get a pail of water. When she returned the fire was burning brightly and the shiny pots and pans twinkled and sparkled so gayly in the firelight, poor Joanleen was sure the house was on fire. Without a word, she pushed the dresser over on the floor, breaking all the dishes to bits and bending and cracking all the wonderful shiny pots and pans.

When Donaleen came home that evening, there was no dinner on the table and the house was a sight. And Joanleen as usual was sitting on the hob with her apron over her head crying for all she was worth. This time Donaleen didn't wait for any explaining. The cut of the house and the loose stone on the hearth told their own story.

"I'll stay here no longer," said Donaleen and walked out the door.

"Where are you going?" wailed poor Joanleen, taking the apron off her head.

"I don't know," said Donaleen, over his shoulder. "But I know I can't live here any longer. Was a man ever cursed with anything worse than a stupid wife."

"Oh wait, wait," cried Joanleen. "I can't stay here alone. I'm coming with you."

"As you wish," said Donaleen. "Pull the door out after you."

So Joanleen wrapped her shawl about her head and then took the door off its hinges. Away they went up the mountain—Donaleen ahead and Joanleen behind, dragging the door after her. Now, they hadn't gone very far when Donaleen stopped and looked around. Indeed, he couldn't imagine what was making all the rattling and banging on the stony road behind him.

"Now, what in the world have you there?" said he to poor Joanleen.

"The door, of course," said Joanleen, beginning to cry again. "You told me to pull it out after me."

I needn't tell you Donaleen was at the end of his patience this time.

"Well, bring it along," said he, finally. "It might come in handy, who knows."

Now Joanleen and Donaleen had never been up on the mountain before and when darkness came on they soon found they had lost their way.

"There is no use wandering around the mountain in the dark," said Donaleen. "Let us put the door up in this big tree and sleep on it for the night." It was no sooner said than done and when they had both climbed up it was not long before they were fast asleep.

Now, as luck would have it, three rogues who had been up to no good business that night, gathered under the tree to divide their loot. They emptied their bags of treasure out on the ground and it shown brightly in the pale light of the rising moon.

Meanwhile, Donaleen and Joanleen slept away as sound as ever and their snoring soon began to echo and re-echo among the rocky crags high above their heads. Indeed, the mountainside was soon filled with such strange noises, the three rogues were sure they were surrounded and made off down the mountain as fast as their legs could carry them.

The next morning when Donaleen and Joanleen climbed down from the tree, there was the treasure scattered about on the ground—gold and silver and jewels galore. In the light of the rising sun, they were fairly dazzled with the sight of it. Well, I needn't tell you, they piled it all to the last penny on top of the door and soon found their way back to their cabin.

And that is the end of my story—
So put on the kettle and make some tay,
And if they didn't live happy—well, we may.

LITTLE DERMOT AND THE THIRSTY STONES

On the southern coast of Ireland there is a series of long rocky headlands that stretch far out into the wild Atlantic like the fingers of a great hand. On one of these headlands there stands a group of upright stones and many wiser heads than yours or mine have wondered whether they were placed there by man or nature.

Like many other strange rock formations in that part of the island they are avoided by the people of the fishing village nearby at the foot of the cliff. For, like anything that is strange and unusual, the stones are considered the haunt of the good people of the fairy world.

Now one time in the fishing village there lived a little orphan boy and his name was Dermot. Dermot was a sweet-tempered, kindly little fellow who earned his few pennies a day minding herds of cows and goats on the meadows that stretched about the standing stones.

Little Dermot did not fear the strange rock formations that rose abruptly from the windswept meadows. Indeed he considered the stones his truest and most loyal friends, and had a name for each one of them. For to Dermot each stone had a personality all its own.

If the sun was nice and warm he would sit with his back against one of the stones and feel the warmth of its rough surface through his threadbare jacket. And if a cold west wind whipped in from the sea he would sit on the east side of one of the widest stones and watch the great Atlantic flecked with white beneath the stormy sky as it stretched far to the distant horizon.

On the outskirts of the fishing village there stood an ancient tumbledown cottage that looked as if it had weathered many a storm from the west. And within its crumbling walls there lived an old woman who looked as ancient and weatherbeaten as the dwelling itself. She was indeed so ancient her features looked for all the world like a wrinkled old potato, and her clothes were so tattered and torn the children of the village called her Biddy the Rags.

Biddy's temper was so violent and her curse so powerful everyone kept well out of her way I can tell you. If any-one should meet her by accident on her comings or goings he treated her with due respect for she was supposed to be in league with the fairy people.

Many times when little Dermot would be sitting at the foot of the great stones he would see Biddy the Rags wan-dering by herself over the fields. Sometimes when he was driving his herds to the village at night he would see her sitting in the shelter of a ditch with the wild birds and small animals of the fields gathered about her while she fed them crumbs from the little sack of bread she always carried at her side.

One stormy night when the west wind was blowing the waves of the Atlantic mountains high, two black crows settled on the roof of Biddy's cottage. While they stood near the chimney for a bit of warmth, the old woman, who understood their language, heard them talking.

"It's a wild night," said one crow to the other.

"It is then," said the second. "Did you hear about the stones?"

"What stones?" said the first.

"The stones on the cliff of course," said the second.

"Well, what about them then?" said the first.

"Now it's strange that you haven't heard," said the second crow. "Why tomorrow night at midnight the standing stones will rush down to the sea and quench their thirst."

"Quench their thirst," exclaimed the first crow. "Now what kind of a cock-and-bull story is that? Whoever heard of stones quenching their thirst?"

"Upon my word it's a fact," said the second crow. "I got it from a very reliable authority. Every hundred years the stones quench their thirst in the sea. And would you believe it, there is a great treasure lying under each of those stones."

"Then what's to prevent someone helping himself while the stones are away?" said the first crow.

"Nothing at all, nothing at all," said the second. "But I also heard the treasure would crumble to dust if a supreme sacrifice isn't made when the treasure is taken."

"Well in that case it's just as well no one knows anything about it," said the first crow. And with that the crows flew off to their rookery leaving Biddy the Rags huddled by the fire in a state of such excitement over what she had heard that she scarcely closed an eye the rest of the night.

For hours on end the old woman tumbled and tossed, and when morning came she had a selfish, bloodthirsty plan worked out, a plan that would keep her share of the buried treasure from crumbling into dust and make her the richest woman in all the land.

So up she climbs to the top of the cliff bright and early and tells little Dermot of the great happenings that would take place that night. And if he would be on hand and not say a word to a soul he would be the richest boy in all Ireland.

Oh it's a grand story she gave him about what a fine lad he was and the only one in the whole village that was worthy of the treasure. She also told him a grand story about how well she knew his parents and how fond they were of her and how grieved she was when they were shipwrecked at sea during a great storm.

Of course little Dermot never suspected the old creature and promised to be on hand at the midnight hour.

During the bright sunny afternoon, however, while Dermot sat with his back against one of the stones he began to think a little more seriously about the whole matter and wished he hadn't made such a hasty promise to the old woman.

After all, the standing stones were his oldest and truest friends so why should he rob them when they were quenching their thirst after a hundred years of waiting.

It was a bit strange too, Dermot decided, that the old

woman should wish to share her great secret with a poor little boy like himself.

Little Dermot had just about made up his mind to ignore the old woman entirely when a tiny little creature no more than a foot high suddenly appeared from behind one of the stones and stood directly in front of him.

The little creature was dressed in a green costume the likes of which Dermot had never seen and it carried in its hand a long rush.

"I've been reading your thoughts, young fellow," said the little creature in a tiny musical voice. "Come at midnight as the old woman bids, for your old friends the standing stones will be glad to share their treasure with you. But mind, do exactly as I say. Go down to the bottom of the cliff and break off a good length of honeysuckle vine that you will find growing there and place it around the base of the stone that is directly behind your back. When the stones are away be sure to jump into the hole left by this stone and no other. Farewell now until we meet again."

At that, the strange little creature with the rush was gone in a flash. Dermot went down to the bottom of the cliff and broke off a good length of the honeysuckle vine and placed it around the standing stone as the little creature had suggested.

Well a few minutes before midnight little Dermot and Biddy the Rags arrived at the top of the cliff.

The old woman was in the best of spirits and smiled at Dermot with her toothless gums and patted him on the head and had just begun to tell him another made-up story about his parents when suddenly there was a great hollow sound like the roar of distant thunder. In the pale light of the stars they could see the great stones wrench themselves from the earth, leap across the meadows in great bounds, and as suddenly disappear over the edge of the cliff.

Without another word Biddy the Rags rushed to the spot where the stones had been and leaped into one of the holes.

Little Dermot could see the honeysuckle vine lying on the ground where he had placed it and when he looked into the hole he could hardly believe his eyes. The bottom was filled with a glittering treasure that sparkled faintly in the pale light of the stars.

Dermot jumped quickly into the hole and no sooner had his cap and pockets filled with pieces of gold and silver and precious jewels when he could hear the stones scrambling up the side of the steep cliff.

Dermot reached for a tuft of grass at the edge of the hole above his head but it gave way when he tried to pull himself up the steep side.

Suddenly the little creature with the rush appeared at the edge of the hole and quickly lowered the honeysuckle vine over the edge.

Dermot grasped the vine and, as thin and weak as it was, and as tiny as the little creature was, Dermot was pulled out of the hole just as the great stones came bounding across the meadow.

In the next minute the great stones were once more in place and Biddy the Rags, in her selfishness, forgot about the time.

Well, I needn't tell you the sacrifice was made and Dermot's treasure never turned to dust and he grew up to be one of the best loved and richest men in all Ireland.

THE TWO BOTTLES

ONCE UPON a time in Ireland, when the little people were more frequently seen than in these unbelieving times, a farmer named Pat O'Brien rented a few acres of barren ground in the neighborhood of the beautiful city of Cork.

Now Pat had a wife and family, but his children were all too young to give him much help with his work, and so the poor man soon found he had great difficulty in paying his rent. Then there came a bad year when the little grain of oats was all spoiled and the chickens died of the pip and the blight ruined the potatoes. Poor Pat found he hadn't enough money to pay even half the rent when it was due.

"Why then, Bridget," says Pat to his good wife, "now what'll we do?"

"Wisha then," says his wife, "what would you do but take the cow to the fair at Cork and sell her? Now Monday is fair day and that's tomorrow."

"And what'll we do when she's gone?" says Pat sorrowfully.

"Never a know I know, Pat," says Bridget, "but sure God won't leave us without Him."

About twelve o'clock the next day then, Pat left for the fair, getting a fair warning, you may be sure, not to sell his cow except for the highest penny.

Pat promised to mind and went his way along the road. He drove his cow slowly before him across a wide stretch of barren country. When he finally reached the top of a high hill, quite suddenly a man overtook him.

"Good morrow," says the man in a high shrill voice.

"Good morrow kindly," says Pat, turning around at the stranger.

The man was a little fellow, so small indeed you would almost call him a dwarf, and yet he wasn't quite so small either. He had an old, wrinkled, yellow face, for all the world like a dried cauliflower. His nose was long and sharp, and his hair was long and white. His eyes were never quiet, but seemed to be looking everywhere at once with such a strange expression that made Pat feel quite cold

all over when he looked at them. Pat couldn't see a bit of his legs or body, for although the day was warm he was all wrapped up in a big overcoat.

"Where are you going with the cow, honest man?" asks the old fellow.

"To the fair at Cork then," says Pat, trembling at the shrill, piercing tones of the voice.

"Are you going to sell her?" asks the stranger.

"Why then, what else am I going for but to sell her?" says Pat.

"Will you sell her to me?" says the little fellow.

Pat started. He didn't want to have anything to do with the little man and yet he was afraid to say No.

"What'll you give for her?" at last says Pat.

"I'll tell you what, I'll give you this bottle," says the little man, pulling a bottle from under his coat.

Pat looked at him and the bottle and, in spite of his terror, he could not help bursting into laughter.

"Laugh if you will," says the little man, "but I tell you this bottle is better for you than all the money you will get for the cow in Cork. Yes, ten thousand times as much."

"Why, then," says Pat, laughing again, "do you think I am such a fool to give my good cow for a bottle, and an empty one at that! Indeed then, I won't."

"You had better give me the cow and take the bottle or you'll be sorry for it," says the little fellow.

"And what would Bridget say?" says Pat. "I'd never hear the end of it. And besides, how would I pay the rent? And what would we all do without a penny of money?"

"I tell you, this bottle is better for you than money. Take it and give me the cow. I ask you for the last time, Pat O'Brien."

How does he know my name? Pat thought, as the stranger went on.

"Pat O'Brien, I know you well, and I have a regard for you. Therefore, do as I warn you, or you will be sorry for it. How do you know but your cow will die before you get to Cork?"

Still Pat hesitated.

"Well then, good-by," says the little man, with a grin that made him look ten times uglier than ever. "I can stay no longer. Once more, take the bottle and be rich; refuse it and beg for your life, see your children in poverty and your wife dying for want. I warn you that will happen, Pat O'Brien."

"Maybe it's true," says Pat, still hesitating. He could hardly help believing the old man and yet he felt he shouldn't be too hasty. At last he grabbed the bottle.

"Take the cow," says he, "and if you are telling a lie, the curse of the poor will be on you."

"I care nothing for your curses or your blessings, but I have spoken the truth, Pat O'Brien, and that you will find out tonight if you will do as I tell you."

"And what's that?" says Pat.

"When you go home," continues the stranger, "never mind if your wife is angry, but be quiet yourself, and make her sweep the room clean, set the table out right, and spread a clean cloth over it. Then put the bottle on the table with these words: 'Bottle, do your duty,' and you will see what you will see."

"And is that all?" says Pat.

"No more," says the little man. "Good-by, Pat O'Brien, you will be a rich man."

"God grant it," says Pat and started homeward. But when he turned back to have another look at the purchaser of his cow, the little old man and the cow were nowhere to be seen.

"Lord between us and harm!" thinks Pat. "He can't belong to this world."

Pat hurried home, holding the bottle carefully under his coat for fear it should be broken, and worrying a bit about what his wife would say. He found her sitting by the turf fire in the big chimney when he entered the kitchen.

"Oh, Pat, are you come back?" cries Bridget. "Sure you weren't all the way to Cork. Where is the cow? Did you sell her? How much did you get for her? Tell us everything about it."

"Why then, Bridget," says Pat, sitting down, "if you'll give me time, I'll tell you all about it. But if you want to know where the cow is, it isn't Pat can tell you, for indeed he doesn't know where she is now."

"Oh, then you sold her," says Bridget delightedly. "And where is the money?"

"Arrah, stop awhile, Bridget," says Pat a bit shyly, "and I'll tell you all about it." But when he had told her what had happened, his poor wife was thunderstruck.

"Oh, Pat," she cried, "I never thought you were such a fool. What'll we do for rent now?" And she burst into a flood of tears.

When Bridget stopped crying and scolding, Pat gave her the instructions about the floor and the table. Then she got up without saying a word and began to sweep the earthen floor with a bunch of heather.

When she had tidied up everything and spread her only clean cloth on the long table, Pat then placed the bottle on the table and said these words, "Bottle, do your duty."

No sooner were the words from his lips than two tiny little fellows rose like light from the bottle and in an instant covered the table with dishes and plates of gold and silver full of the finest food that ever was seen. When all this was done they disappeared as quickly into the bottle again.

Pat and his wife looked at everything with astonishment. They had never seen such plates and dishes before in their lives. Indeed, they were speechless with amazement and all they could do was walk around and around the table.

"Come and sit down, Pat," says Bridget when she finally could speak. "Let's try to eat a bit. Sure you ought to be hungry after such a good day's work. The little man told you no lie."

Pat finally sat down, after calling the children from the loft, and they all made a hearty meal, though to be sure they couldn't taste half the dishes.

"Now," says Bridget when she had eaten all she could, "I wonder will the two good gentlemen carry away these fine things again." They all waited, but no one came, so Bridget put everything away carefully into the dresser.

When Pat and his wife and children finally went to bed, they were full of plans about selling the fine dishes that they did not really want.

So the very next day Pat took some of the plates to Cork City and with the money bought a horse and cart and some clothes for himself and his family. Indeed from that day out Pat's fortunes took a decided turn for the better. His children grew fat and healthy from good food, and the grand appearance of the whole family displayed at church on Sundays was the envy of the neighbors.

The children were warned by their father not to say a word to a soul about the bottle, but children will be children and wiser heads than theirs soon had the secret out of them. In time Pat's landlord got wind of the bottle and of course by hook or crook nothing would do him but he must have it at all costs. The landlord offered Pat a deal of money for it, but Pat wouldn't give in till at last the landlord offered to let him keep his barren bit of land rent free, so Pat, who never thought that he would want any more money now that he was so rich, gave the landlord the bottle.

But Pat was mistaken. He and his family spent money as if there were no end to it and quickly became poorer and poorer, till at last they had nothing left but one cow. So Pat once more drove her before him to sell at Cork fair, hoping to meet the old man and get another bottle.

It was hardly daybreak when he left home and he walked

on at a good pace, driving his beast before him, till he reached the big hill where he had met the little man.

When Pat reached the summit of the hill, he stopped for a moment to enjoy the prospect around him. Suddenly he was overjoyed to hear the same, well-known voice.

"Well, Pat O'Brien, I told you you would be a rich man."

"Indeed then," says Pat, so delighted he could scarcely speak, "sure enough I was, that's no lie for you, sir. But it's not rich I am now. Have you another bottle, good sir, for I want it now as much as I did long ago. If you have it, sir, here is the cow for it."

"And here is the bottle," says the old man, smiling. "You know what to do with it."

"Oh, then, sure I do," said Pat, taking the bottle.

"Well, farewell forever, Pat O'Brien."

"Good-by to you, sir," said Pat turning back, "and good luck to you. Good-by, sir, good-by."

So Pat walked back as fast as he could, never looking after the little white-haired gentleman and the cow, so anxious was he to bring home the bottle.

Well, he arrived with it safely enough and called out as soon as he saw Bridget, "Oh, sure I've another bottle."

"Arrah then, have you?" cried Bridget overjoyed. "You

are a lucky man, Pat O'Brien, that's what you are."

In an instant she put everything to rights, and Pat, looking at his bottle, cried out, "Bottle, do your duty." In a twinkling two great stout men with clubs issued from the bottle. Around the house they flew, breaking this and breaking that, knocking a head here and a leg there, and then as suddenly vanished into the bottle again.

Pat's poor family sat on the floor in amazement, rubbing their wounds and looking about at the cut of the house. All the dishes and windows were broken, and the pots and pans and ashes from the fireplace were scattered everywhere.

Well, the secret of Pat's second bottle never got beyond the cottage door, I can tell you.

Now in a few days the landlord, who was in possession of the first bottle and making good use of it, you may be sure, gave a grand party at his house and invited all the gentry of the country round. When Pat heard all the music and laughter and saw the windows of the fine house ablaze with lights, he was more than ever aware of how he had foolishly let untold wealth slip through his fingers.

While Pat was thinking on all this, he suddenly had an idea. So without a word to his family he put the second bottle under his coat and hurried across the fields and spacious lawns and knocked at the landlord's door. A servant opened the door and asked him what he wanted.

"His lordship, sir," says Pat.

"His lordship is very busy tonight," says the servant. "I'm afraid he will not be able to see you."

"Well, just tell your master Pat O'Brien has come with another bottle," says Pat, knowing very well that would do the trick.

"A bottle," says the servant in disgust. "What would his lordship want with your bottle? Be off with you."

"Oh, he'll be interested enough," says Pat. "Just say the word 'bottle' and tell him who brought it."

The servant finally agreed to deliver the message, and sure enough the landlord appeared in short order. He led the way to a private room at the top of the house where the other bottle was kept. Pat then drew the second bottle from under his coat.

"Why, it's exactly like the other," says the landlord rubbing it greedily with his hands. Then, taking the first bottle out of its place of safety, he placed the two bottles side by side. "Now tell me, has the second bottle the same power?" asks the landlord.

"Oh indeed, your honor," says Pat, "it has twice the power. Shall I give you a sample?"

The landlord, so excited to see what would happen, readily consented. So Pat gave the command, "Bottle, do your duty." In the next instant the landlord was tumbling on the floor and the ladies and gentlemen and servants all over the house were running and roaring and sprawling and kicking in a frightful manner. The two huge men laid about them without mercy until the entire house was upset and wreck and ruin was on every side.

Pat meanwhile placed the first bottle carefully inside his jacket and, when the two men had vanished again into the second, he placed that one also carefully in his pocket.

Well, I needn't tell you Pat made good use of bottle number one and soon he was living again in the best of style. His son in time married the landlord's beautiful daughter and the wedding party was such a grand affair that it was the talk of the countryside roundabout for many years afterward.

SHAUN AND THE MERMAN

ON THE wild and rocky coast of southern Ireland, there once lived a young man with his wife, and his name was Shaun O'Casey.

If you ever saw the wild and desolate headland on which their cottage was built, you would wonder, indeed, why the Caseys had picked such a lonesome place. Great rocks were scattered all about, and there was nothing to look at but the great Atlantic, stretching far to the west. There was a little creek near-by where Shaun kept his boat and, directly before the cabin, a long ledge of sunken rocks stretched far out into the sea.

Now it was this very ledge of sunken rocks that made the lonely spot a desirable place to live, for when the Atlantic, according to custom, was roaring with a storm, many's the richly laden ships that were blown to pieces on the sunken rocks. Then the fine bales of cotton and tobacco and casks of brandy would be washed ashore. Why, bless you, the wild and rocky point was as profitable to the Caseys as would have been the richest estate in all of Ireland.

Although Shaun had been a bit of a hermit all his life, he was, all-in-all, a good-natured fellow. That is why his good wife, Bridget, left her comfortable home in Skibbereen to live with him on this wild and lonely shore, with only seals and gulls for neighbors. Bridget was no fool and knew a good man when she saw one. And, after all, didn't she have the best to eat and drink, and didn't she put in the best appearance at Chapel on Sundays?

Now you may be sure it was many the strange sights and many the strange sounds that Shaun experienced in his business with the sea. But he was a bold and fearless fellow, and nothing ever daunted him. Shaun had often heard of the mermaids and mermen that were supposed to be as thick as lobsters along that particular part of the coast, but try as he would he never saw one.

Shaun had heard they were mighty pleasant creatures and that luck had always come with an acquaintance with one of them. What really vexed Shaun more than anything else was that both his father and grandfather, who were the first of his family to settle on the lonely point, had often seen them. His grandfather had even struck up a very intimate acquaintance with a merman, and luck and good fortune had followed him to his grave.

Now, one day while Shaun was strolling a little farther than usual along the coast, he saw something, like nothing he had ever seen before, perched on a rock a little distance out at sea. Its body was green, as well as he could make out, and it had, of all things, a cocked hat under its arm. Shaun stared and stared a good half hour at least, and all that time the thing on the rock never stirred hand or foot. At last Shaun's patience was at an end. He gave a loud whistle and the merman (for that is what it was) suddenly put the cocked hat on its head and dived straight down into the sea.

Well, Shaun's curiosity was aroused, you may well be sure, but as many times as he revisited the spot he never caught another glimpe of the sea gentleman with the cocked hat. Indeed, Shaun soon began to think that perhaps the whole experience had been a dream.

One very rough day, however, when the seas were running mountain high, Shaun determined to have another look at the merman's rock, to see if the creature would return in stormy weather. There, sure enough, it was, cutting capers on the top of the rock and then diving down into the waves and coming up again.

"I must get acquainted with him at all costs," said Shaun to himself, and so, on the next blustering day, he walked to the rock. But as the tide was in and the sea running high, he had to take shelter in a cave along the shore. Shaun had no more than entered the cave when, to his amazement, he saw sitting before him a thing with green hair, long green teeth, a red nose, and eyes like those of a pig. It had a fish's tail, legs with scales on them, and short arms like fins. It wore no clothes, but a cocked hat was held firmly under its arm.

Shaun with all his courage was a little daunted, I needn't tell you; but pulling himself together, he walked up to the merman, took off his cap, and made his best bow.

"Your servant, sir," says Shaun.

"Your servant, kindly, Shaun O'Casey," says the merman.

"To be sure now, how well you know my name," said Shaun.

"I know your name?" replied the merman. "Why, man, I knew your grandfather long before he was married to your grandmother. Ah, Shaun, my boy, I was indeed very fond of that grandfather of yours. I never met his match above or below for tossing off a shellful of brandy. I hope you're his own grandson."

"Never fear me for that," said Shaun.

"Good lad," said the merman, smiling. "You and I must get better acquainted, if it's only for your grandfather's sake."

"I'm sure," said Shaun, "since your honor lives down under the water, you must be obliged to drink a powerful lot to keep any heat in you. Now, may I be so bold as to ask you where you get the stuff?"

"Where do you get it yourself?" asked the merman, with a knowing wink.

"Oh, I see how it is," said Shaun, smiling. "But I suppose your honor has a fine dry cellar below to keep it in. I am sure it must be mighty well worth looking at."

"You may say so, Shaun," said the merman, "and if you will meet me here next Monday at this time of day, we shall have a little more talk with one another about the matter."

So Shaun and the merman parted the best of friends. On the following Monday they met as planned, and Shaun was a bit surprised to see that the merman had two cocked hats with him, one under each arm.

"May I be so bold as to ask you, sir," said Shaun, "why your honor brought two hats with you today, instead of one?"

"Well, Shaun," said the merman, "I want you to come down and eat a bit of dinner with me, and I brought you the hat to dive with."

"The Lord preserve us," cried Shaun in amazement. "Do you want me to go down to the bottom of the sea? Sure I'd be smothered and choked with water, to say nothing of being drowned."

"Now, indeed," said the merman, a little out of patience, "your grandfather would never have talked that way. Many's the time he stuck this hat on his head and dived down boldly after me, and many's the good dinner and shellful of brandy we had together."

"Is that so now?" said Shaun. "Well then, here goes. No tricks. Play me fair."

"Ah, that's your grandfather all over," said the merman. "So come along, my boy, do as I do."

They both left the cave and swam a piece until they came to the rock. The merman climbed to the top and Shaun followed him.

"Now put on this hat," said the merman, "and mind you keep your eyes open. Take hold of my tail and follow after me and then you'll see what you'll see." Into the sea dashed the merman and Shaun after him.

Down, down, down they went and Shaun thought they would never stop going. Shaun held on tightly to the merman's slippery tail and, at last, to Shaun's surprise, he found himself on dry land at the bottom of the sea.

They landed just in front of a neat little house that was slated with oyster shells. Shaun was so surprised he couldn't speak, you may be sure, and he was out of breath from traveling so fast through the water.

All about him were crabs and oysters walking leisurely on the sand, and overhead was the sea, with fishes swimming about in it.

"Why don't you say something?" said the merman. "I dare say you had no notion that I had such a snug little spot as this."

"No, indeed," said Shaun when he finally got his breath, "but who in the world would ever have thought of such a thing."

"Well, come along, my lad," said the merman, "and let's see what they have for us to eat."

Shaun was really hungry and he was indeed glad to see

a fine column of smoke rising from the chimney. Into the house he followed the merman and there he saw a grand kitchen, well provided with everything. There was a dresser and pots and pans, and two young mermen, cooking. The old merman then led Shaun into a room where a good fire was blazing on the hearth.

"Come now, and I'll show you where I keep—you know what," said the merman with a sly look; and opening a door he led Shaun into a fine cellar filled with kegs and hogsheads and barrels.

"Well, what do you say to that, Shaun O'Casey?" said the merman. "Maybe a body can't live snug down under the water, eh?"

"No doubt of that at all," said Shaun.

So, back into the room they went and found the table laid. And what a feast was laid before them! There were oysters and lobsters, and turbot, and sole, and at least twenty other kinds of fish that Shaun had never heard of. At least a dozen bottles of varied spirits stood in the center of the table. When Shaun and the merman sat down, they ate and drank 'til they could hold no more.

Then Shaun said, helping himself to another shellful of brandy, "Well, here's to your health, sir, and may you live these fifty years."

"Fifty years," repeated the merman. "Now if you had said five hundred it would be something worth wishing. One lives to a powerful age under these waters. Don't forget I knew your grandfather when he was a lad and he is dead now some sixty years. But come, my lad, keep the liquor stirring."

So shellful after shellful they drank and, to Shaun's great surprise, his head kept very cool while the merman got very mellow and sang many songs, but for the life of him Shaun couldn't remember a one of them afterwards.

"Now, my dear boy, if you'll follow me I'll show you my curiosities," said the merman, and he led the way into a large room where things like lobster pots were arranged on shelves along the wall.

"Well, Shaun, what do you think of them?" said the merman.

"Well," said Shaun finally, "if I may be so bold as to ask, what are they, sir?"

"Soul cages," said the merman. "These are what I keep the souls in."

"What souls?" said Shaun in amazement. "Sure the fish have no souls."

"Of course they haven't," said the merman. "But these contain the souls of drowned sailors."

"The Lord preserve us from all harm," said Shaun. "How did you get them?"

"Easily enough," said the merman. "When a ship is wrecked on the rocks above, I place these pots about, and when the souls escape from the drowned bodies they are glad to take shelter in the pots. After that it's easy to fetch them home and here I keep them dry and warm. Now isn't it well for poor souls to get such good quarters?"

Shaun was so thunderstruck he didn't know what to say, so he said nothing. Back they went to the dining room, had some more brandy, and then Shaun said he thought it was time for him to be on the road.

"Just as you like, my boy," said the merman, and after they had a parting glass the merman placed one of the cocked hats on Shaun's head the wrong way and then lifted him up on his shoulders until he reached the water above his head.

"Now," said the merman, "you'll come up at just the spot you came down and mind you throw me back the hat."

Like a shot Shaun rushed up through the water and, when he reached the rock, threw back the hat, which sank like a stone.

Now Shaun never said a word to Bridget about his adventure, but the state of the poor souls in the pots gave him no end of worry. After a few days, he finally hit upon a plan to free the souls. He would ask the merman to dinner at the cottage, make him as sleepy as possible on poteen, a mixture Shaun had made himself out of potatoes and sugar, and then take the hat and go down and turn up the pots.

First of all he had to get Bridget out of the way, so it's very pious he got all of a sudden. He suggested to his wife that it would be good for both their souls if she were to make a pilgrimage to a local shrine a few miles distant. Bridget thought it was indeed a grand idea and off she set one morning at daybreak.

As soon as the coast was clear, away went Shaun to the rock, tossed a stone into the water, and in the next minute up sprang the merman.

"Good morning, Shaun," said the merman. "What do you want with me?"

"Nothing much, sir," said Shaun. "But, since my wife is away for the day, I wonder if you would come and take potluck with me?"

"Agreed," said the merman. "What's the hour?"

"Say, one o'clock," said Shaun, "and then you can go home with the daylight."

"I'll be with you, never fear," said the merman as he

put on his hat and disappeared below the waves.

So Shaun went home and laid out a noble fish dinner and brought out his best poteen.

"That's the lad that will settle him," said Shaun to himself, patting the bottle. "I'll bet that rascal, as old as he is, never saw a drop of poteen in his life."

Just to the minute the merman came with his cocked hat under his arm and, as dinner was ready, down they sat and ate and drank manfully.

"And pray, sir, how do you like the poteen?" asked Shaun finally.

"It's good stuff," said the merman. "Where does it come from?"

"Oh, that's a secret," said Shaun. "But it's the real stuff. Believe me, sir, it's fifty times better than brandy, or rum, either."

The poteen was indeed the real stuff and the merman was delighted with it. He drank and sang and danced and finally fell to the floor, fast asleep. With a wink at the success of his scheme, Shaun snapped up the cocked hat, ran to the rock, leaped in, and soon arrived at the merman's house.

All was still and quiet. Not a merman, old or young, was about, so Shaun quickly turned up the pots to free the souls of the drowned sailors. As he lifted each one of them, he could see nothing, but was quite sure he heard a little whispering sound. At this Shaun was not surprised, for he had often heard the priest say that no one could see the living soul, no more than they could see the wind or air.

Having done all he could for the poor souls, Shaun set the pots as they were before, and once more put the hat the wrong way on his head. But when he got out of the room, he found the water so high above him he had no way of reaching it without the merman to give him a lift. He walked about looking for a ladder or something he could stand on but nothing could he find. At last he saw a spot where the water hung lower than anywhere else and just as he reached it a big codfish happened to put down his tail. With a good jump Shaun grabbed the tail, and the codfish in amazement gave a bounce and pulled Shaun up toward the surface. The instant the hat touched the water, Shaun was whisked up like a cork and reached the rock in no time at all.

Now meanwhile, Bridget had arrived home a little earlier than usual.

"Well, here's a nice how-to-do," said she, when she saw the state of the house with food and empty poteen bottles scattered all about. "While I'm away saying prayers for

our souls, here is my fine lad at home, drinking our best poteen with some old crony."

Suddenly there was a loud grunt and when Bridget looked under the table, there was the merman fast asleep. "The Blessed Virgin save me," she cried. "I have often heard of a man making a beast of himself with drink and here, upon my word, is the real thing."

Out of the house she ran in a fright and in the next minute heard the well-known voice of her Shaun, singing a merry tune as he came up from the shore.

Bridget was so delighted to see him, she quickly forgave him the cut he had made of the kitchen, and then, of course, Shaun had to tell her everything.

When they returned to the cottage, Shaun woke the merman, who soon made off with himself. He didn't have the good manners even to say good-night.

Now I have been told that the merman never missed the souls and he and Shawn always remained the best of friends. As for Shaun, I needn't tell you, luck and good fortune followed him the remaining days of his life.

THE THREE SNEEZES

WELL, it all began one warm sultry evening in summer when young Tim McCarthy was returning from a harvesting at his good neighbor's, John Malone, at the other side of the mountain.

Young Tim was in a pleasant jovial mood since the latter part of the evening had been spent with good talk and good food and good drinking.

The ham that John's wife had prepared for supper, however, was a bit on the salty side, so as Tim walked leisurely along the thirst of the day was still upon him.

"Faith, a jug of good beer would hit the spot this minute," said Tim aloud to himself.

The words were no sooner out of his mouth when a husky voice sounded from the side of the ditch.

"Never say it twice, me lad. Never say it twice."

Tim was a bit startled, you may be sure, and when he looked around there stood a queer-looking little man no more than three feet high, with a long black beard and a fine foaming mug of beer in one hand.

The little fellow offered the mug to Tim, and Tim, not being in a very questioning mood at the moment, took the mug and tossed off the beer at one swallow.

"Thank you kindly, sir," said Tim wiping the foam from his lips and returning the mug. "A better glass of beer I've never tasted."

Tim was about to continue his way when the little fellow suddenly caught him by the suspender.

"Hold on now," said he. "Not so fast, me young bucko. That will cost you exactly a shilling."

"A shilling for a little mug of beer," laughed Tim, not realizing at the moment he wasn't talking to a fellow mortal. "Be off with you, you little half pint. I could get two honest-sized mugs of beer in any public house for the same price. Is it for a fool you take me?"

"But not at the moment you need it most," said the little fellow flying into a rage. "You'll regret this day, Tim McCarthy. Follow me."

At that the strange little man set off across the bog that stretched along one side of the road and Tim, unable to control his feet, followed after. Up one side of the long dreary bog they wandered and then down the other, into pools of stagnant water one minute and around stacks of drying turf the next, until the glow of a new day finally appeared in the eastern sky. At last the little man turned around suddenly and said, "For a year and a day, Tim McCarthy, you shall do my bidding. This night has been only a sample. Farewell then, until we meet again."

At that the little man vanished and Tim, weary with his day's labor and his night's aimless tramping, went home as quickly as he could and managed to get a few winks of sleep before returning to work.

Well, the next day Tim wasn't much help at the harvesting, I can tell you, and while he was returning home in the evening the little man again appeared at the very same spot. Without so much as a "Good evening," he commanded Tim to go into the bog and pluck two bull rushes. Away went Tim into the bog, without any will of his own, and plucked two of the largest bulrushes he could find growing at the edge of a pool of black bog water.

"Now do as I do," said the little man, taking one of the rushes and placing it between his legs, "and we will be off."

Tim felt a bit of a fool placing the thin rush between his legs but he had no sooner done so when the little fellow muttered something in his beard, and before Tim knew what was happening he was sitting on a great white horse and the little man was sitting on another just beside him. With another strange muttering the horses were off at lightning speed over highland and lowland and woodland and bog-land. Poor Tim had unfortunately put the wrong end of the rush between his legs so that he sat backward on the horse and had to grasp its flowing tail to keep from falling off. On and on they flew with the swiftness of the wind till they came to a beautiful house that stood in the center of a dense wood. At once the little man dismounted and commanded Tim to do likewise.

"Here is one of the best stocked kitchens in all of County Kerry," said the little fellow. "Follow me, my lad, and we will have a night of it."

Without another word the little man leaped through the keyhole of the great door and without any trouble at all Tim was able to do the same.

They now found themselves standing in a beautiful room, but the little man didn't give Tim a moment to admire the grand furnishings when he leaped through another keyhole and then another with Tim right at his heels.

At last they came into a great vaulted room with meats and pastries and bottles of milk and honey arranged on shelves along the wall. Without any more ado the little fellow began to help himself to the first thing at hand and bid Tim to do likewise.

Well, they ate and drank until they could hold no more and at the first crowing of the cock the little fellow gave Tim a wink and then with a dash was through the keyholes again with Tim close behind. With a leap the little man was on his horse and when Tim was on his, face forward this time, they were off with the speed of the wind.

Now on the second night it was the same story. Tim gathered the rushes and away they flew on white chargers to feast in some far off kitchen. But on the third night the little man commanded Tim to pluck three rushes instead of two.

"Now what will you do with the third?" said Tim as he placed one of the rushes between his legs.

"Well," said the little man, "I am a thousand years old tonight and I am thinking very seriously of getting married."

"If you are going to get married at all," said Tim, "you should have your mind well made up by this time. Who is the bride?"

"Wait and see," said the little fellow with a wink, and when he muttered the strange words and the horses were beneath them, another white charger was standing alongside. Away again they flew over woodland and bogland with the third horse following close behind. This time they stopped in front of a simple farmer's cottage where a wedding party was taking place.

When the little fellow and Tim dismounted they went into the cottage and the little man at once climbed to one of the rafters and bid Tim to do likewise. The little man seemed quite comfortable on his high perch with his legs tucked under him as tidy as a tailor, but poor Tim felt very foolish perched on the rafter with his feet dangling over the people's heads.

Now from his high position Tim noticed the little man on the rafter opposite was keeping a close eye on all that was going on beneath him. He watched the bride, a beautiful girl of about eighteen, with particular interest.

In the midst of all the merriment the bride suddenly sneezed, but as everyone about her was so busy dancing or eating or talking or listening to the music no one said "God bless us." At that, the little man on the rafter squeezed himself with glee and watched the young bride more closely than ever.

Again the bride sneezed but this time she managed to cover it in a handkerchief so no one heard her. At that the little man squeezed himself tighter than ever and Tim could hear him muttering to himself, "Once more and she is mine. Once more and she is mine."

Now Tim watched the bride very closely and when she sneezed for the third time Tim shouted at the top of his lungs, "God save all here."

At that the face of the queer little man on the rafter opposite turned as black as soot and the next minute he was off the rafter and out the door. Well, I needn't tell you the spell was broken and Tim McCarthy never saw the little fellow and his white horses again as long as he lived.

THE POOKA

ONCE upon a time in a little coastal town of southern County Cork there lived an old couple who had one son and his name was Michael.

Now Michael was a restless, headstrong lad and when he had reached his fifteenth year he became weary of the simple humdrum life of the village. Without a word to his parents he ran away to Cork City and in a few days got employment on a ship sailing for America.

Well, time passed as time will, and with the passing of the years Michael came into a modest fortune in the new world.

With money now in his pocket, Michael had a great desire to see his parents again and revisit the scenes of his early childhood.

On his return to the little village of his birth, he stopped into a tavern to make a few inquiries about his parents, for he had not written a single letter to them during his years in America.

The proprietor of the tavern was glad to see Michael again, for he was an old friend of the family, but he was indeed sorry to have to tell the young man that his parents had both died shortly after he had run away to sea.

Michael was so grieved at this sad news he vowed he would make a pilgrimage to the blessed chapel of St. Gobnate and make atonement for his sins.

It was still early in the afternoon, so he decided to leave at once.

Now the chapel was situated in a wild and desolate place, and the shortest route was directly over the top of a near-by mountain.

For a good two hours Michael climbed the rocky slope, winding his way in and out between boulders as big as houses, with patches of woodland on one side and swampy bogland on the other.

When Michael reached the summit of the mountain, he

soon found himself enveloped in a dense fog that had suddenly rolled up from the other side. The fog was indeed so thick, and the daylight was fading so rapidly, Michael soon lost his way. He sat down on a near-by stone for a few minutes to get his bearings.

He had no sooner seated himself when a bright light appeared a little way off in the direction of the chapel, as Michael thought at the moment.

"It's a farmer's cottage," said Michael to himself. "And I am sure there will be someone there who will be able to show me the right path to the chapel."

He rose quickly and walked toward the light, but the light did not grow any brighter. As he walked along it still seemed to be the same distance before him.

A strange dizziness came over him as he stumbled along between the rocks and clumps of briars and heather that grew in his path.

Michael sat down again and for a moment covered his face with his hands until the feeling had passed.

When he glanced at the light again it was now like a great ball of fire and so near that Michael could see the form of an old woman, wrapped in a long black garment, sitting beside it.

She was holding something in her hands which she tore

savagely with her teeth and when she caught sight of Michael standing in the glow cast by the ball of fire she seemed annoyed to be disturbed at her meal.

"Good evening, ma'am," said Michael surprised, you may be sure, at the strange appearance of the old creature.

"What do you want?" growled the old woman, and suddenly her eyes seemed to shine like green lights in her dark features.

Michael explained his mission and said he had lost his way in the fog and darkness.

He had no sooner stopped speaking when the old woman, with her shining eyes still upon him, stood up and began to move away. Michael felt strangely compelled to follow her and, as they walked along, the old creature never for a moment took her eyes off him.

On and on they went over bog and moorland, with the great ball of fire moving alongside and lighting the way.

At last they came to a rocky cliff that rose in front of them like a great wall. The old woman picked up a stone from the ground and hit the rocky cliff. She had no sooner done so when a hollow sound like a roll of thunder was heard and one section of the cliff slowly opened like a door and a huge white horse suddenly appeared and stood by her side.

"Here is a horse to take you to your destination," cried the old creature and with superhuman strength she caught Michael about the waist and placed him on the back of the huge beast. Then, with a wild shriek of laughter, the old women threw her arms above her head and the horse leaped forward into the darkness with Michael grasping its great flowing mane.

The next morning, on a lonely strand many miles from Michael's village, a fisherman found Michael lying at the foot of a high rocky cliff. His body was covered with cuts and bruises, and he was in such a dazed condition he didn't realize what had happened to him for many days afterward.

"You met the Pooka, me lad," everyone said and, when Michael finally could recall the details of his adventure on the mountain, he agreed that they were right. Indeed Michael often wondered afterwards why he had met the Pooka on that particular night. But I have told my story, so you can draw your own conclusions.

CLEVER TOM AND THE LEPRECHAUN

ONCE upon a time in Ireland there lived a young lad and his name was Tom O'Leary.

He was the son of a comfortable farmer and as clever, industrious, and good-looking a young fellow as you could find in a day's journey.

One fine day in harvest (it was a holiday), Tom was taking a ramble for himself through his father's fields. He went sauntering along the sunny side of a ditch, thinking to himself what would be the harm if people, instead of idling away the day, were to shake out the hay and bind and stook the oats, when all of a sudden he heard a clacking sort of noise just a little way in front of him.

"Dear me," said Tom to himself, "but isn't it now really surprising to hear the stone-chatters singing so late in the season."

So Tom stole along the side of the ditch, going on the tips of his toes to see if he could get a sight of what was making the noise and make sure that he was right in his guess.

The noise suddenly stopped but, as Tom looked sharp through the bushes, what did he see in the shadow of a sloe bush but a brown pitcher that might hold about a gallon and a half, and by it a tiny old man with a little cocked hat stuck on the top of his head and a dusty leather apron hanging down before him.

Suddenly the little man stood up on the stool he had been sitting on and dipped a little ladle into the pitcher. He put the ladle to his lips and, when he had drained it to the last drop, he went on with his work, putting a heelpiece on a bit of a brogue that might have fitted himself, it was that small.

"Well by the powers," said Tom to himself, "I often heard tell of the leprechauns and, to tell the God's truth, I never believed in them but here is one in earnest. Now if I go knowingly to work I am a made man. They say a body must never take his eyes off them or they will escape."

Tom stole a little farther with his eyes fixed on the little man just as a cat does with a mouse.

"God bless your work, honest man," says Tom when he got quite close to him.

"Thank you kindly," says the maneen.

"I wonder you'd be working on the holiday," says Tom.

"That's my own business and none of yours," was the reply, short enough.

"Well, you may be civil enough then to tell me what you have in the pitcher there," says Tom.

"That I will, with pleasure," says the little man. "It's good beer."

"Beer," says Tom. "Blood and turf, man, where did you get it?"

"Where did I get it?" says the leprechaun. "Why I made it, to be sure. And what do you think I made it of?"

"Malt, I suppose," says Tom. "What else!"

"It's there you are out," says the little man. "I made it of heather."

"Of heather," says Tom bursting out laughing. "Sure now, you don't think me such a fool to believe that. I wasn't raised under a duck."

"Do as you please," says the little man, "but what I tell you is the real truth. Did you never hear of the Danes?"

"To be sure I did," says Tom. "Weren't they the chaps that got such a licking when they tried to take Ireland from us?"

"Hum," says the little fellow dryly. "Is that all you know about the matter?"

"Well what more about them then?" says Tom.

"You're a very ignorant young fellow," says the little man. "It's easy to see that. Why, when the Danes were here they taught us to make beer out of the heather and the secret has been in my family ever since."

"Would you give a body a taste of your beer to try?" says Tom.

"I'll tell you, young man," says the maneen. "It would be much more fitting for you to be looking after your father's property than to be bothering decent quiet people with your foolish questions. Now while you are idling away your time here, the cows have broken into the oats and are knocking the corn all about."

Tom was so taken by surprise at this that he was just on the point of turning around, when he suddenly collected himself. So afraid he was that the like might not happen again he made a grab at the leprechaun and caught him up in his hand. In his hurry he overset the pitcher and spilled the beer, so he never found out what it really tasted like.

Tom then looked at the little fellow with a blood-minded look in his eye and swore he would kill him outright if he didn't show him where all his money was hidden.

Indeed the little fellow was so frightened he began to whimper and cry.

"So," said he finally. "Come along with me across a few fields and I'll show you where you can find a crock of gold."

Away they went over hedges and ditches and crooked bits of bog. Indeed the leprechaun seemed, out of pure mischief, to pick out the hardest and most contrary way. Tom never took his eyes off the little fellow for one instant until at last they came to a field full of thistles. The leprechaun pointed to a big thistle that grew near the middle of the field.

"Dig under that," said the little man, "and you'll get a crock full of golden guineas."

"I'll have to run home for a spade," said Tom very excited, and at that took off one of his red garters and placed it around the thistle so he would know the very spot when he returned.

"Well, I suppose you have no further occasion for me," said the leprechaun very civilly.

"No," said Tom. "You may go away now if you like,

and God speed you and luck attend you wherever you go."

"Well, good-by to you, Tom O'Leary," said the leprechaun smiling. "And much good you may do with what you get."

So Tom ran home for the spade as fast as he could and then back to the field of thistles. When he reached the field he could hardly believe his eyes. Lo and behold, there wasn't a thistle in the field that didn't have a red garter hanging about it, the very identical model of his own.

Tom stood for a moment scratching his head. To dig up the whole field was out of the question, for there were twenty or more good Irish acres in it. So Tom put the spade on his shoulder and went home again, a bit cooler, you may be sure, and it's many the hearty curse he gave the leprechaun.

THE STRANGE LITTLE PIPER

ONCE UPON a time in Ireland, and a very good time it was, there lived in the County of Cork a decent honest couple whose names were Michael O'Donovan and Mary Malone. These poor people were blessed, as the saying goes, with four children, all boys. Three of them were as fine, stout, healthy, good-looking children as ever the sun shone upon. Indeed, it would make any Irishman proud to see them, about noon on a fair summer's day, standing at their father's cabin door with their beautiful fine flaxen hair curling about their heads, their cheeks like two rosy apples, and a big laughing potato smoking in their hands.

A proud man was Michael of these children, and a proud woman too was Mary, and reason enough they had to be so. Yet I am sorry to say that the fourth child, which was the oldest, gave them no end of worry. The bright light of golden sunshine seemed to radiate from the three younger children, but the darkness of night seemed to have settled in the heart and appearance of the fourth. His skin was dusky; his hair was black; and his eyes, though large and beautiful, had a strange expression. He never learned to walk as the other children did, and so he never left his cradle.

The neighbors all agreed that the little dark creature had been left by the fairies, and that the real baby had been taken in his place to the little people's mountain haunts shortly after he was born. "Wisha Mary, why don't you give him the water test?" they would often ask the poor mother. "Take him across a rushing stream and, if he behaves strangely, you may be sure he's no mortal child."

But Mary, who dearly loved the child, would listen to none of it. "Oh, that's only an old superstition," she would always say. "The child is all right, never fear!"

Yet, when all the country people got about the fire of a winter's evening and began to talk of religion and good things, the little fellow as he lay in his cradle would begin to cry so loudly, and throw his arms and legs around in such an angry fashion, it was plain to see he was very displeased with the trend of the conversation.

Well, things went on in this way for some time, until one day Tim, the blind piper, going his rounds, happened in to warm himself by the fire and have a chat with the woman of the house. After a bit, when he had a cup of tea and a bit of soda bread that Mary had just baked, he yoked on his pipes and began to bellows away in fine style. The minute the music began, the little brown-eyed fellow lying in his cradle suddenly sat up and tossed his arms and legs about in high glee.

At last nothing would do him but he must get the pipes into his own hands and, to humor him, Mary asked Tim to let the child have the pipes for a minute. Tim, who was kind to children, readily consented, and as Tim hadn't his sight, Mary herself brought the pipes to the cradle. She was about to put them on the child, but she had no need, for the fellow was quite up to the business. He buckled on the pipes, set the bellows under one arm and the bag under the other, and worked them both as knowingly as if he had been twenty years in the business. In the next minute he lilted up "The Hare Was in the Corn" in the finest style that ever was heard.

Well, I needn't tell you all was amazement. Mary, the poor woman, crossed herself; and Tim, not knowing who was playing, was in great delight. When he heard, however, that it was a child not yet eight years old, who never had seen a set of pipes in all his days before, he wished the mother joy of her son. He offered to take him off her hands, swearing he was a born piper, a natural genius, and declaring that in a little more time, with a little help from himself, there wouldn't be his match in the whole country around.

The poor woman was greatly delighted to hear all this, particularly when Tim said the child was a natural genius, for it put an end to some misgivings that had been rising in her own mind, after what the neighbors had been saying about the little fellow. Now her child wouldn't in time have to be forced out into a cruel world, but would be quite capable of earning decent, honest bread for himself.

So when Michael came home in the evening from his work, she up and told him all that had happened and all that Tim the piper had said. Michael, of course, was very glad to hear it, for the helpless condition of the little fellow was a great worry to him. On the next Fair Day he sold the pig, and with the money bought a brand new set of pipes, the proper size for the youngster.

The minute that the little fellow clapped his eyes on the

pipes, he fairly squealed with delight; and when they were buckled on, he pulled away with "The Rocky Road to Dublin," to the admiration of all who heard him.

Well, the fame of his skill on the pipes soon spread to far and near, for there wasn't a piper in the next three counties who could hold a candle to him, as the saying goes. To hear him rattle away "The Fox Hunt," you really would have thought you could hear the hounds giving tongue and the huntsmen cheering or correcting the dogs. It was, indeed, the very next best thing to seeing the hunt itself.

The little piper was in no way stingy with his music, and many's the merry dance the boys and girls of the neighborhood used to have in his father's cabin, and he would play up music for them that would put quicksilver in their feet. Everyone declared that he never moved so light and airy to any such playing in all his life.

But, besides all his fine Irish music, the little piper had one queer tune, one of his own, the oddest that ever was heard, for the minute that he began to play it, everything in the house seemed to dance. The plates used to jingle on the dresser, the pots and pot hooks used to rattle in the chimney, and people used to fancy that they felt the stools moving from under them. Whatever way it may have been with the stools, no one could sit on them for long when that tune was played, for both old and young always fell to capering as hard as ever they could.

The girls complained that when the piper began that tune they never could handle their feet rightly, for they felt the floor like ice under them, and themselves ready every minute to come sprawling on their backs or their faces.

The young men, who wanted to show off their dancing, swore that the tune confused them so that they could never go rightly through the heel-and-toe, or cover-the-buckle, or any of their best steps, but felt themselves always bewildered and wanting only to go jostling and knocking one another, up one side of the room and down the other, in a frightful manner.

Now the older the little piper grew, the greater effect his music seemed to have, and by the time he was nine years old there was no staying in the same house with him. He was always having his brothers dancing about the house, barking their shins on the stools, or scalding and burning themselves at the fire. One time in harvest he was left alone by himself, and when his mother came in she found the cat, the dog, the goat, and the goose, dancing about the house like mad. Another time when the mother was coming in from milking the cow, with the pail on her head, the little fellow struck up his queer tune. When the poor woman

put her hands to her sides and broke into a jig, down tumbled the pail of milk and spilled all over her husband, who was bringing in some turf for the supper fire.

Soon afterward, the farmer whom Michael was working for began to have no end of misfortune, and he was sure that Michael's strange little piper was the cause of all the mischief. A fine calf died of the black-leg, a horse took the staggers, and some cows acted so wild that they wouldn't let anyone milk them; and, for no reason at all, the roof of the cowhouse suddenly fell in.

One day the farmer called Michael aside and said to him, "Michael, you see that things are not going well with me, and to be plain and honest with you, I think that child of yours is the cause of it. I am really falling away to nothing with fretting, and I can hardly sleep at night for thinking of what may happen before the morning. So I'd be glad if you would look for work somewhere else. You're as good a man as any in the whole county, and there is no fear you will find your choice of work."

Michael said that indeed he was very sorry, and to tell the truth, he wasn't so easy in his own mind about the child. As much as he hated to go, he would see about looking for work somewhere else in the next few days.

So on the next Sunday at chapel, Michael told his friends

that he was looking for work somewhere else. And at that, a farmer who lived a couple of miles off came up to him and said he wanted a ploughman, and Michael could have a house and garden and all the work he wanted the year around. Michael knew that the man would be a good employer, so he closed the deal. The farmer said he would send his cart to take Michael's little bit of furniture on the following Thursday.

When Thursday came, the cart appeared according to the farmer's promise, and Michael loaded it, placing the cradle with the child and his pipes on top. Mary sat beside the cradle to take care of the little fellow. The dog followed in the road, and of course the cat would not leave the house and had to be left behind. The other three children went along the road picking blackberries, for it was a fine day toward the latter part of harvest.

Now they had to cross a river, but as it ran between two high banks, they didn't see it until they were very close to it. The little piper was lying quietly in the bottom of his cradle till they came to the head of the bridge, but when he heard the roar of the water, he sat up suddenly in his cradle and looked about him. When he saw the water and found that his parents were going to take him across it, he began to wail so loudly that, indeed, you wouldn't have thought he was equal to it.

"Whist, now!" said Mary, trying to quiet the little fellow. "There's no fear. Sure, it's only over a stone bridge we are going."

But the farther they got over the bridge, the louder the little one cried, and when his mother tried to comfort him again, he suddenly rose up in the cradle and, with his pipes under his arm, hopped over the battlements of the bridge and down into the water. The poor mother screamed, and Michael and the other children rushed to the other side of the bridge, but when they reached the river's edge, they stopped in amazement. From beneath one of the arches of the bridge, they could see the little piper sitting tailor-wise on top of a white wave, playing away his strange tune as if nothing had happened at all.

The river was running very hard, so he was whirled along at a great rate, but he played as fast as the river ran. Michael and the other children set off as hard as they could along the river bank. But as the river made a sudden turn about a hundred yards below the bridge, the little piper was out of sight by the time that they got there and no one ever saw him again or heard his strange music.

"Ochone! Ochone!" cried the poor mother. "The neighbors were right. He was a fairy child, and we should never have brought him across the rushing water. He is gone back to his own people now, and it's fine music that he'll be making for them."